OWL MOON

by Jane Yolen

illustrated by John Schoenherr

SCHOLASTIC INC.

NEW YORK   TORONTO   LONDON   AUCKLAND   SYDNEY

ISBN 0-590-42044-5

Text copyright © 1987 by Jane Yolen.

Illustrations copyright © 1987 by John Schoenherr.

All rights reserved. Published by Scholastic Inc., 730 Broadway, New York, NY 10003, by arrangement with The Putnam Publishing Group.

50 49 48 47 46 45   1 2/0

Printed in the U.S.A.   08

First Scholastic printing, September 1988

For my husband, David,
who took all of our children owling —J.Y.

To my granddaughter, Nyssa,
for when she is old enough to go owling. —J.S.

It was late one winter night,
long past my bedtime,
when Pa and I went owling.
There was no wind.
The trees stood still
as giant statues.
And the moon was so bright
the sky seemed to shine.
Somewhere behind us
a train whistle blew,
long and low,
like a sad, sad song.

I could hear it
through the woolen cap
Pa had pulled down
over my ears.
A farm dog answered the train,
and then a second dog
joined in.
They sang out,
trains and dogs,
for a real long time.
And when their voices
faded away
it was as quiet as a dream.
We walked on toward the woods,
Pa and I.

Our feet crunched
over the crisp snow
and little gray footprints
followed us.
Pa made a long shadow,
but mine was short and round.
I had to run after him
every now and then
to keep up,
and my short, round shadow
bumped after me.

But I never called out.
If you go owling
you have to be quiet,
that's what Pa always says.

I had been waiting
to go owling with Pa
for a long, long time.

We reached the line
of pine trees,
black and pointy
against the sky,
and Pa held up his hand.
I stopped right where I was
and waited.
He looked up,
as if searching the stars,
as if reading a map up there.
The moon made his face
into a silver mask.
Then he called:
"Whoo-whoo-who-who-who-whooooooo,"
the sound of a Great Horned Owl.
"Whoo-whoo-who-who-who-whoooooooo."

Again he called out.
And then again.
After each call
he was silent
and for a moment we both listened.
But there was no answer.
Pa shrugged
and I shrugged.
I was not disappointed.
My brothers all said
sometimes there's an owl
and sometimes there isn't.

We walked on.
I could feel the cold,
as if someone's icy hand
was palm-down on my back.
And my nose
and the tops of my cheeks
felt cold and hot
at the same time.
But I never said a word.
If you go owling
you have to be quiet
and make your own heat.

We went into the woods.
The shadows
were the blackest things
I had ever seen.
They stained the white snow.
My mouth felt furry,
for the scarf over it
was wet and warm.
I didn't ask
what kinds of things
hide behind black trees
in the middle of the night.
When you go owling
you have to be brave.

Then we came to a clearing
in the dark woods.
The moon was high above us.
It seemed to fit
exactly
over the center of the clearing
and the snow below it
was whiter than the milk
in a cereal bowl.

I sighed
and Pa held up his hand
at the sound.
I put my mittens
over the scarf
over my mouth
and listened hard.
And then Pa called:
"Whoo-whoo-who-who-who-whooooooo.
Whoo-whoo-who-who-who-whoooooooo."
I listened
and looked so hard
my ears hurt
and my eyes got cloudy
with the cold.
Pa raised his face
to call out again,
but before he could
open his mouth
an echo
came threading its way
through the trees.
"Whoo-whoo-who-who-who-whooooooo."

Pa almost smiled.
Then he called back:
"Whoo-whoo-who-who-who-whoooooooo,"
just as if he
and the owl
were talking about supper
or about the woods
or the moon
or the cold.
I took my mitten
off the scarf
off my mouth,
and I almost smiled, too.

The owl's call came closer,
from high up in the trees
on the edge of the meadow.
Nothing in the meadow moved.
All of a sudden
an owl shadow,
part of the big tree shadow,
lifted off
and flew right over us.
We watched silently
with heat in our mouths,
the heat of all those words
we had not spoken.
The shadow hooted again.

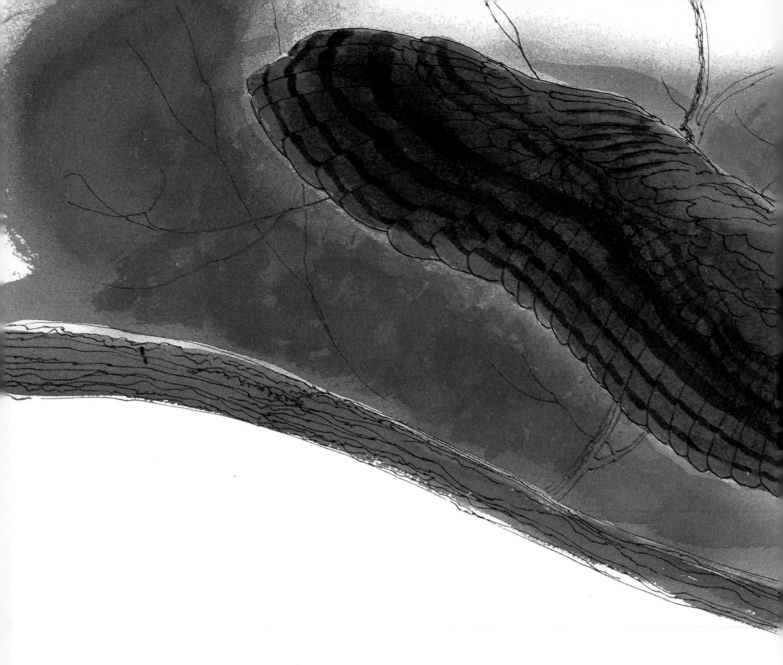

Pa turned on
his big flashlight
and caught the owl
just as it was landing
on a branch.

For one minute,
three minutes,
maybe even a hundred minutes,
we stared at one another.

When you go owling
you don't need words
or warm
or anything but hope.
That's what Pa says.
The kind of hope
that flies
on silent wings
under a shining
Owl Moon.

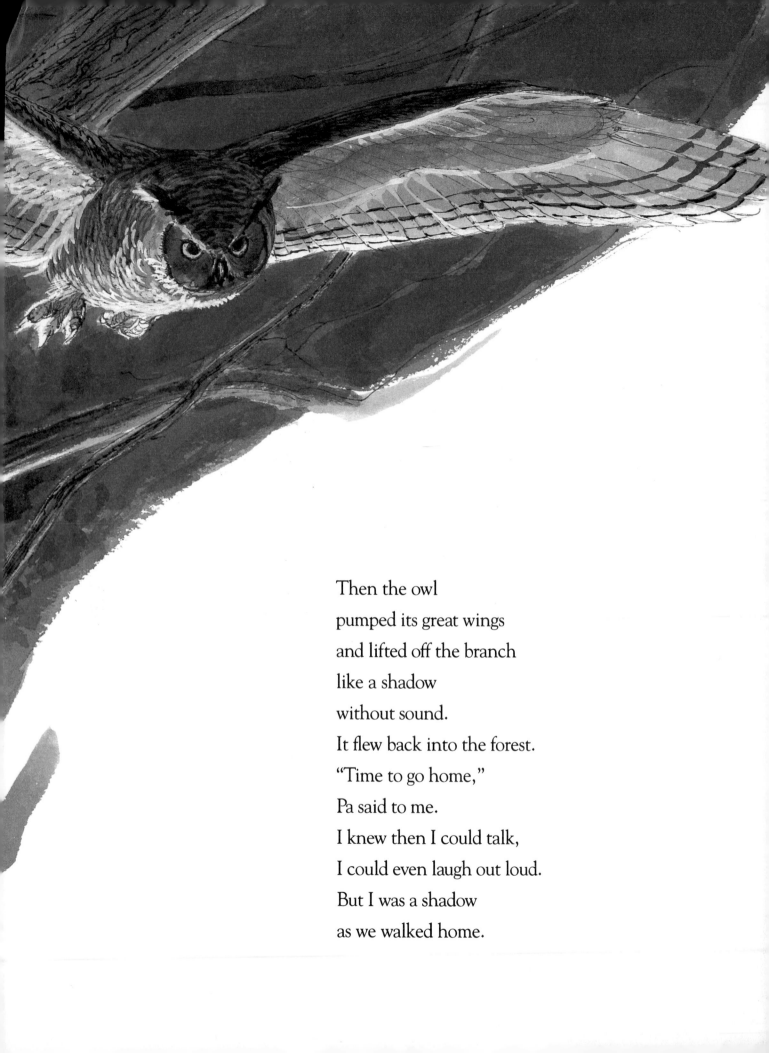

Then the owl
pumped its great wings
and lifted off the branch
like a shadow
without sound.
It flew back into the forest.
"Time to go home,"
Pa said to me.
I knew then I could talk,
I could even laugh out loud.
But I was a shadow
as we walked home.